Dora's WORLD Adventure Storybook

adapted by Ruth Koeppel

based on the original teleplay by Valerie Walsh

Contents

Reader's Digest
Children's Books®

Pleasantville, New York • Montréal, Québec • Bath, United Kingdom

 FRIENDSHIP DAY

DISC 1

1

"Today is Friendship Day!" Dora announced. "**¡El Día de la Amistad!**"

On Friendship Day, friends from all around the world dress up, have parties, and wear special Friendship Bracelets," said Dora.

"When we wear our Friendship Bracelets," Dora explained, "it means that we'll be friends forever."

"Forever and ever?" asked Boots.

Dora nodded.

Boots bounced up and down excitedly. "Dora, I want to see the Friendship Bracelets! Can I, can I?" he asked.

Dora lifted the lid off a box. It was filled with beautiful, glowing Friendship Bracelets.

"Look! Our friends are coming to celebrate Friendship Day with us!" said Dora. "**¡Hola, amigos!** Hi!"

Benny, Isa, and Tico were just as excited as Dora and Boots about Friendship Day.

"When all our friends wear their special Friendship Bracelets," Dora told them, "the bracelets will glow and rainbow sparkles will light up the sky!"

"Wow!" the friends cried. "**¡Qué lindo!** How beautiful!"

Suddenly, there came a sneaky, creeping sound.

"Uh-oh," said Dora. "That sounds like Swiper the Fox."

"There he is!" said Boots, pointing to Swiper zipping through the air in his Swipercopter.

Swiper flew his Swipercopter right at the box of bracelets. Before anyone could stop him, Swiper swiped the box of bracelets and held it up in the air. "You're too late! Ha ha ha!" he laughed.

Swiper was about to empty the box of bracelets into his sack when Dora said, "Swiper, wait! Without Friendship Bracelets, we can't have Friendship Day. I even have a bracelet for you!"

"Uh oh," he said, opening his sack. "I've been flying all around the world, swiping bracelets. I didn't know they were Friendship Bracelets."

FRANCE   **TANZANIA**   **RUSSIA**   **CHINA**

Boots ran over to look inside the box of bracelets. The bracelets no longer glowed.

"The bracelets won't glow unless all our friends around the world have one," said Dora. "Our friends need their Friendship Bracelets!"

"Oh mannn!" said Swiper. "I better give back these Friendship Bracelets."

Swiper climbed in his Swipercopter and pressed the start button, but there was a *clink, sputter* and *boink* as it broke down.

"Don't worry, Swiper," said Dora. "We can return all the Friendship Bracelets together!"

3

"We need to go all the way around the world to bring the Friendship Bracelets back to our friends!" said Dora. "Map! Where do we go to bring back all of the Friendship Bracelets?"

Map flew out of Backpack's pocket. "To bring back the bracelets, first you go to the Friendship Parade at the Eiffel Tower in France, then Mount Kilimanjaro in Tanzania, then up to the Winter Palace in Russia, and then to the Great Wall of China."

"The Eiffel Tower is way across the ocean. How are we going to get there?" Dora asked, staring out to sea.

Just then, a steamer ship sailed up to the dock.

"A really big boat can take us across the ocean to the tower!" said Dora. She asked Boots to stay behind with Benny, Isa, and Tico, and wait for her to get back for their Friendship Parade, and then Dora boarded the ship with Swiper.

EXPLORING FRANCE

DISC 1

The ship pulled up to a dock. "We're in France, Swiper!" Dora said. She changed into a red, white, and blue outfit—the colors of the French flag.

Dora and Swiper made their way through gently rolling hills and vineyards to the edge of a city—Paris!

"Hey Dora, I can see the tower!" said Swiper.

Dora and Swiper were about to head toward the tower when a girl called out, "Dora, Dora!"

Dora and Swiper walked down a street filled with little shops selling bread, pastries, and silk scarves as they waved to the girl.

"It's my friend Amelie!" Dora cried, kissing Amelie on both cheeks. "**Bonjour!** This is Swiper."

"**Bonjour!**" said Amelie. "Dora, everyone's at the tower for the Friendship Parade, but there are no Friendship Bracelets!"

Swiper held up his sack. "I've got the bracelets right here," he said.

"Follow me, quickly!" said Amelie.

Dora and Swiper followed Amelie around a bend and came upon two cobblestone streets.

"Uh-oh!" said Swiper. "I wonder which street we need to take to the Tower."

"To get to the Eiffel Tower, my **maman** told me that the smiling gargoyle can help us," said Amelie.

4

DISC 2

5

"Gargoyle?" said Dora.

One of the gargoyle sculptures carved into the stone buildings came to life.

"**Oui!** I am the gargoyle! **Bonjour!** To find the tower, take that street!" it said, pointing out the street with the circles on it.

"Thanks!" said Dora. "C'mon!"

Dora, Swiper, and Amelie followed the street and reached the Eiffel Tower. It was decorated with balloons for Friendship Day. A crowd of French children waited there.

6 "Dora, I've just gotta give back these Friendship Bracelets!" said Swiper. He poured the bracelets from his sack into the friendship box.

"Bracelets for everyone!" said Amelie, passing out the bracelets.

7 Swiper and Dora handed out the bracelets to Amelie and the other children. They smiled and slipped them on.

Dora waved a bunch of red, white, and blue balloons and everyone cheered.

"Where do we go next?" Swiper asked.

"To the mountain," said Dora. "Mount Kilimanjaro. There's a scooter that can give us a ride."

Dora and Swiper ran to the scooter and hopped on.

"Don't forget your safety helmets!" said Amelie." So you can be safe."

Dora and Swiper buckled their helmets.

"Thanks for bringing the bracelets back!" Amelie said, as the friends kissed good-bye.

"Friends help friends," said Dora.

"Good luck, Swiper!" said Amelie.

"C'mon, we've got to bring the Friendship Bracelets back to save Friendship Day!" said Dora. "**¡Vámonos!** Let's go!"

Dora and Swiper sped off on the scooter out of Paris and headed south to Spain. At the Straits of Gibraltar, the scooter turned into a water scooter to take them to Africa. Then it turned back into a land scooter for the ride across the North African desert.

EXPLORING TANZANIA

DISC 1

1

"Dora, I see Mount Kilimanjaro!" said Swiper.

"Me too, Swiper," said Dora. "We made it to Tanzania in Africa!"

The scooter dropped off Dora and Swiper at a Tanzanian Masai village. The village sat on the edge of the Serengeti Plains with Mount Kilimanjaro in the distance.

2

Dora changed from her French outfit into a colorful Masai dress with a beaded necklace. She was ready to explore Africa!

A boy rode by on an elephant. "Dora, Dora!" he cried.

Recognizing him, Dora smiled. "It's my friend, N'Dari," she said. "**Jambo**, N'Dari! Hello!"

"**Jambo**, Dora!" said N'Dari, as he stopped under a sign marking the entrance to an animal park. "All the kids are at the mountain for the Friendship Parade, but we don't have any Friendship Bracelets."

"I've got the bracelets right here," said Swiper.

"Great," said N'Dari. "To get to the mountain quickly, we have to take a safari through the animal park."

N'Dari pointed at the sign and added, "Along the way, we can see wild animals like hippos, giraffes, zebras, and lions."

"Oooool!" said Dora and Swiper.

4 "Hop on my elephant and we will ride through the animal park!" said N'Dari.

The elephant kneeled down, and Dora and Swiper climbed aboard, and then set off into the animal park.

DISC 2

5 Dora, Swiper, and N'Dari rode the elephant through the park past all the animals.

6 After they left the animal park, Dora, Swiper, and N'Dari made it to the base of the mountain. The elephant bent down so they could climb off his back. A crowd of Tanzanian children ran up to them.

7 "Hey we made it to Mount Kilimanjaro!" said Swiper. "Now I can give the Friendship Bracelets back."

Swiper ran to the bracelet box and poured bracelets into it.

N'Dari called to the children, "Come get your Friendship Bracelets."

Dora and Swiper handed out the **8** Friendship Bracelets to N'Dari and the other children. The crowd clapped and cheered.

"Where do we go next, Dora?" asked Swiper.

"The Winter Palace in Russia," said Dora. "But it's so far away."

Just then, a hot-air balloon floated toward Dora and Swiper.

"We can ride the hot-air balloon to the Winter Palace," said Dora.

"That'll get us there fast!" said Swiper.

The hot-air balloon landed beside them and the two scrambled in.

"Thank you for bringing back the Friendship Bracelets!" N'Dari said, as he waved good-bye.

"Friends help friends!" said Dora, as the balloon lifted off.

"Come on, we've got to bring back the Friendship Bracelets to save Friendship Day! Let's go! **¡Vámonos!**"

EXPLORING RUSSIA

DISC 1

The hot-air balloon floated over a Russian city. "Dora, I see the Winter Palace," said Swiper. "That means we made it to Russia!" said Dora.

The balloon set down near the Winter Palace. Dora and Swiper climbed out and looked around at the snow-covered buildings.

It was very cold! Dora changed from her Tanzanian dress into a Russian coat, hat, woolen mittens, and snow boots. Now she was ready to explore Russia!

As Swiper and Dora walked they passed some friendly people who smiled and said, "**Preev-yet**."

"**Preev-yet**," answered Dora. "To say hello in Russian, we say '**preev-yet**'."

Dora and Swiper heard a bell chime.

"We've got to get to the Winter Palace fast," said Dora.

"So I can give back the bracelets before the parade!" said Swiper.

Swiper marched off, but the snow was so deep, he couldn't go very fast.

"Uh...Dora, it's hard to walk in all this snow," said Swiper.

"Yeah!" said Dora. "We need something to get over the snow quickly. Let's look in Backpack. Backpack!"

Out of Backpack flew a book, a rolling pin, an ice-cream cone, and two pairs of skis.

"Oh! We can use the skis to ski over the snow to get to the Winter Palace," said Dora.

DISC 2

5

Dora and Swiper cross-country skiied down the street, swooshing and swooshing until they reached the Winter Palace.

When they reached the gate Dora's friend Vladimir skiied up.

"**Preev-yet**, Dora," said Vladimir.

"**Preev-yet**, Vladimir," said Dora. "This is Swiper."

"Everyone's at the palace waiting for the parade!" said Vladimir, as he lead them through the gate.

27

Dora, Swiper, and Vladimir skiied onto the palace grounds.

 "We've got to bring the Friendship Bracelets back quick!" said Swiper, pouring the bracelets into the box.

"Yay, Friendship Bracelets for everyone!" said Vladimir. "Hoorah!"

 Dora put a bracelet on Vladimir's wrist. Then a crowd of Russian children gathered around Dora, Swiper, and Vladimir as they handed out more bracelets. The crowd clapped and cheered.

Swiper looked in his sack, which still had a few bracelets at the bottom. "Where do we go next, Dora?" he asked.

"The Great Wall of China," said Dora. "But we've got to hurry. Do you see something we can ride to get there?"

A train chugged out from behind the palace.

"Dora, thank you for all your help!" said Vladimir, waving good-bye as Dora and Swiper hopped aboard.

"Friends help friends!" Dora replied.

The train chugged off, carrying them over snowy fields.

8

● EXPLORING CHINA

DISC 1

1

The train traveled across grasslands and rice paddies.

Dora changed from her Russian outfit into Chinese silk as she gazed out the train window.

"To say hello in Mandarin, we say '**knee-how**', Dora explained. "Say **knee-how** to the people we pass in the rice fields, and the pagodas!"

The train reached the Great Wall and Dora and Swiper scrambled off.

"Wow, that's one great wall!" said Swiper.

"But our friends are on the other side of the wall!" said Dora.

Swiper tried to climb the wall but slid down back down.

"Oh mannn. I'll never get over this wall," said Swiper.

"We can't give up now, Swiper," said Dora.

"Dora! Dora!" came a girl's voice. The girl somersaulted through the air and landed next to Dora.

"**Knee-how**, Hello, Mei!" said Dora, playing with a Chinese lantern. "This is Swiper."

"**Knee-how**!" said Mei. "I've been looking for you. We don't have any Friendship Bracelets!"

Swiper held up his sack. "I've got the Friendship Bracelets, but we have to go over the Great Wall to bring them back!"

"To get over the wall, we're going to have to super-jump," said Mei.

"Jump, jump!" cried Dora.

They jumped through the air and sailed over the Great Wall, landing gently on the other side.

5

"Wow!" said Dora. "Great super-jumping!"

Dora, Swiper, and Mei stood in the middle of a crowd of children wearing colorful silk clothing.

"I've got to give back the Friendship Bracelets!" said Swiper.

"Follow me!" said Mei.

6

Mei, Dora, and Swiper held hands as they made their way through the crowd of children.

"Coming through!" cried Mei. "Friendship Bracelets on the way!"

33

7 When they reached the empty bracelet box, Swiper held up the sack and poured the last of the bracelets into it.

"Friendship Bracelets for everyone!" Mei called out.

The crowd cheered and Dora did a special dance with a ribbon, while other children flew kites in celebration.

8 The children lined up, and Dora and Swiper handed out the bracelets.

"We did it!" said Dora. "We brought all the Friendship Bracelets back!"

"Yippee!" cried Swiper, jumping for joy.

The crowd cheered.

"We brought the Friendship Bracelets back to our friends all over the world," said Dora.

"So will the Friendship Bracelets glow all over the world now, Dora?" asked Swiper.

"They should, Swiper," said Dora. "We've got to get back home to Boots to see if they do!"

"Ooo, ooo! We better hurry," said Swiper.

A shiny jet plane rolled over to them.

"Next stop, home!" said Swiper.

"Thank you, Dora!" cried Mei. "You saved Friendship Day!"

"Friends help friends!" said Dora.

She and Swiper ran to the plane and climbed aboard.

BACK AT HOME

DISC 2

1

The jet flew Dora and Swiper home. The plane landed and the crowd swelled around it.

Out of the plane came Dora, wearing a long party dress. By her side was Swiper, wearing a bow tie.

"Yay!" the crowd cheered, waving.

Boots ran up to Dora excitedly. "Dora, you made it, you made it!" he cried. He threw himself into her arms and gave her a big hug.

Benny stepped forward with their box of bracelets. Boots reached in and took one out.

"I gave out almost all the Friendship Bracelets, Dora," said Boots. "This one is for you."

Dora slipped on the bracelet. "Thanks, Boots," she said.

Swiper stepped forward.

"Is there a Friendship Bracelet left for me?" asked Swiper.

Dora reached into the box and slipped a bracelet on Swiper. "This one is for you, Swiper!"

Suddenly, the bracelets started to glow, brighter and brighter. They shot beams of light into the sky. Rainbow sparkles exploded overhead. The happy crowd clapped and cheered.

"We brought back all the Friendship Bracelets and saved Friendship Day!" Dora said. "And now we'll all be friends..."

"...forever and ever!" Dora and her friends finished together. "Hooray!"

"We did it!" Dora cried. "**¡Lo hicimos!**"